D0472491
ON THE STUMP™

★ IMAGE COMICS PRESENTS ★

ON THE STUMP™

FEATURING

CHUCK BROWN
WRITER

PRENZY
ARTIST

CLAYTON COWLES
LETTERER

AND

SANFORD GREENE
VARIANT COVER ARTIST

SHANNA MATUSZAK
EDITOR

WITH ASSISTANCE FROM

JULIAN C. CHAMBLISS
BACK MATTER EDITOR

RYAN BREWER
DESIGN & PRODUCTION

DREW GILL
COVER & LOGO DESIGN

AND ESSAY CONTRIBUTIONS BY

MICHAEL D. KENNEDY
MATTHEW TEUTSCH
MARTIN LUND
KARLOS K. HILL
EMILY J.H. CONTOIS

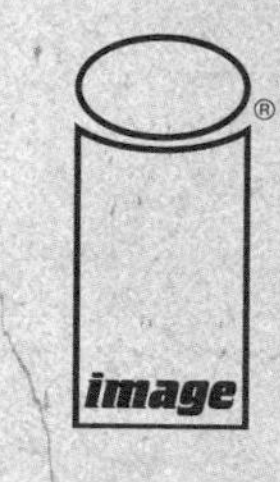

ON THE STUMP. First printing. November 2020. Published by Image Comics, Inc. Office of publication: 2701 NW Vaughn St., Suite 780, Portland, OR 97210. Printed in the USA. For international rights, contact: foreignlicensing@imagecomics.com. ISBN: 978-1-5343-1608-9.

ROUND
1

ALTERNATE COVER BY SANFORD GREENE

WASHINGTON, D.C.
COME ON, AMERICA!! LET'S MAKE SOME MUTHAFUCKING NOISE!!!
YEAAAAAHH!!!
OHH! JACK TAKES A BRUTAL LEFT FROM SHAW!
SENATOR JACK HAMMER
SWEET SMELL IS MURDERING JACK HAMMER OUT THERE!! HAMMER HASN'T THROWN ONE GODDAMN PUNCH, FOLKS!!
SLAM

THAT'S IT, SWEETHEART! LET GO!
SENATOR
SWEET SMELL
SHAW

AAAHHHHHH!
OHHH! THE DEAD HAVE RISEN!

KRACK!!!
OOOF!!
KRACK!!!
SQUISSSK!
KICK!!
IT'S ALLLL OVER, FOLKS!
I'M GONNA KILL YOU, MOTHERFUCKER. I'M GONNA KILL YOU.

YOU HEAR ME?!
YEAH-- I HEAR YA.
IN AN AMAZING UPSET, SENATOR JACK HAMMER DEFEATS SENATOR SWEET SMELL SHAW!! SWEET SMELL'S BILL TO DEREGULATE GENETIC ENHANCEMENT IN THE RING WILL NOT MAKE IT TO THE HOUSE OF REPRESENTATIVES!
AND A LOT OF YOU JUST LOST A SHIT TON OF MONEY! NOW FOR THE NEXT MATCH ON THE STUMP!
A SHIT TON OF MONEY IS AN UNDERSTATEMENT. I'M GONNA HAVE TO WORK MY ASS OFF TO PAY THIS DEBT. JACK HAMMER HASN'T PUT UP A REAL FIGHT IN 20 YEARS! WHY'D THE FUCKER HAVE TO START TODAY?!
SHOW SOME RESPECT. THE HAMMER ONCE FOUGHT A TAG TEAM ALONE FOR TWO HOURS. THE GUY WAS A BEAST IN HIS HEYDAY. BACK WHEN THE POLITICIANS ACTUALLY MENTIONED THE ISSUES BEFORE THE FIGHT.
JACK HAMMER WAS OVERRATED AT HIS PEAK, AND HE'S A LOSER NOW. JUST 'CAUSE HE CAN TAKE A PUNCH, IT DON'T MAKE HIM GREAT.
NOW SWEET SMELL SHAW HAS RAW POWER AND SPEED. HE EXPLODES ON AN OPPONENT AND DOESN'T LET UP TILL THE JOB IS DONE. A LOT LIKE CONGRESSMAN KELLY KILL SWITCH. REMEMBER HIM?
KILL SWITCH WAS A BOXER. HE HAD GRACE AND STYLE. SWEET SMELL IS A BRUISER. THEY'RE NOTHING ALIKE.
FUCK YOU, WHAT DO YOU KNOW?!
I ♥ YOU
SWEET SMELL DIDN'T DO HIS JOB. SO IT'S TIME TO DO OURS.

ARE YOU GONNA HIDE BACK HERE ALL DAY? PEOPLE ARE LOOKING FOR YOU.
BURRITOS
TACOS
SO, LET 'EM LOOK.
YOU HAVEN'T WON A FIGHT IN, LIKE, SIX YEARS. PEOPLE ARE GONNA WANT TO TALK TO YOU. FANS, LOBBYISTS, REPORTERS. SHIT, EVERYBODY!
WRONG, I HAVEN'T WON IN FOUR YEARS.
WRONG AGAIN, YOU HAVEN'T PASSED ANY LEGISLATION IN THE RING SINCE YOU DEFEATED SILVER SABER.
THAT WAS FIVE YEARS AGO.
FOUR--FIVE YEARS--NO ONE GIVES A SHIT.

MR. HAMMER! YOU HAVE TO PAY FOR THOSE.
HERE.
SENATOR HAMMER, I JUST WANT TO TALK.
NO COMMENT. NO AUTOGRAPHS. JUST LEAVE ME ALONE, LADY.
DAMN IT! DON'T WALK AWAY FROM ME!
I HAVEN'T PUNCHED A LADY OUTSIDE THE RING SINCE 2002! DON'T MAKE ME BREAK MY STREAK, BITCH!
AHHHRR!!

YEP, THERE GOES MY STREAK.
UGH!
OOOF!
UGHH!
OK, OK. ONE AUTOGRAPH, BUT IT'LL COST YOU FIVE BUCKS.
MY NAME IS AGENT ANNABELLE LISTER.
I'M WITH THE FBI, YOU IDIOT.
WE NEED TO TALK. IN PRIVATE.

All ambrosia
All the night
Ice Cream
GREEK GOD GRUB
SSSSLURP
SLURP
SQUISH
SLURP
SSSSLURP
WELL?
TALK!
DID YOU KNOW YOU WERE IN THE NEWS YESTERDAY?
WHAT WAS IT THIS TIME? AM I TRAFFICKING DRUGS WITH THE MEXICANS? STEALING MONEY FROM THE ELDERLY IN MY DISTRICT? OR DO I HAVE A LOVE CHILD WITH QUEEN LATIFAH?
MORE LIKE CONSPIRACY TO COMMIT MURDER. YOU WERE SUPPOSED TO DIE IN THAT RING TODAY.
THE ARTICLE SAYS CALIFORNIA SENATOR THUNDER BEARER IS TRYING TO PASS LEGISLATION THAT WILL ALLOW KILLING IN THE RING. YOUR FIGHT WITH SWEET SMELL SHAW *SHOULD* HAVE ENDED WITH YOU BEING BEATEN TO DEATH.
IT WOULD HAVE BEEN THE CATALYST TO MOVE THUNDER'S LEGISLATION FORWARD. HE'S CALLING IT THE SLAY ACT.

NEWS
Legal murder in the ring

COME ON, AGENT. THERE ARE HUNDREDS OF NEWS FEEDS LIKE THIS. JUST TELLING PEOPLE WHAT THEY WANT TO HEAR. WHY ARE YOU WASTING MY TIME ON THIS ONE?
BECAUSE I'VE BEEN INVESTIGATING THUNDER BEARER FOR FIVE YEARS. THIS REPORT CONFIRMS EVERYTHING I'VE LEARNED ABOUT HIM. AND THE SOURCES IN THIS NEWS FEED ARE REAL. THIS IS BIG.
SO, WHAT DO YOU NEED ME FOR?
I'VE SEEN YOU FIGHT BEFORE. SURE, YOU LOSE--A LOT--BUT YOU DIDN'T THROW A SINGLE PUNCH UNTIL THE END. WHY?
FINE. I WAS PAID TO THROW THE FIGHT. BUT I OBVIOUSLY WOULDN'T SIGN UP TO BE SOME SACRIFICE FOR A PIECE OF LEGISLATION. SO ARE WE DONE?
NO. ONE, I NEED A SENATOR I CAN TRUST. TWO, I'M SURE YOU CAN BE TRUSTED SINCE THUNDER WAS PLANNING TO KILL YOU. AND THREE--
AND THREE?
AND THREE, YOU USED TO STAND FOR SOMETHING. YOU ONCE FOUGHT FOR THE PEOPLE, NOT JUST TO ENTERTAIN, COLLECT A CHECK, AND KEEP YOUR SEAT IN THE HOUSE.
SORRY TO INTERRUPT, BUT YOU BROKE A DEAL, JACK. YOU ALSO IMPRESSED THE BOSS, THOUGH. SO--

--YA GET OFF EASY.
AAAHHHHHH!
SON OF A BITCH!
BAM BAM BAM
UUHHRGRRRR
IT'S OK, JACK, I'LL CALL AN AMBULANCE!
JACK, WAIT!
GET BACK HERE!!!

SNIF
SNIFFF
AHH
WHY THE HELL DO YOU DO THAT EVERY TIME WE VISIT A HOSPITAL?
YOU KNOW I LIKE THE SMELL OF HOSPITALS.
BULLSHIT. YOU PRETEND TO LIKE THE SMELL BECAUSE YOU KNOW IT ANNOYS THE SHIT OUT OF ME.
NO.
THAT'S SOMETHING YOU WOULD DO.
THESE PLACES SMELL LIKE OLD RAGS AND BLEACH. HOW IS THAT PLEASANT?
THE SMELL IS IODOFORM.
IODO THE FUCK WHAT??

IODOFORM. IT'S WHAT THEY CLEAN WITH.
THIS IS THE ROOM.
HUH, I SEE YOU WENT WITH THE STETHOSCOPE.
WHAT? TOO MUCH?
TOO MUCH.
LISTEN. I DID MY PART. I PAID JACK HAMMER TO THROW THE MATCH. I CAN'T HELP THAT HE FOUGHT BACK!!
AHHHH SHIT. DUDE, YOU ARE A LEGEND. I WATCHED YOU DEFEND YOUR SEAT AGAINST CONGRESSWOMAN SARA THE SAW IN 2008.
YOU KICKED HER RIGHT IN THE PUSSY. I MEAN WHO DOES THAT?
WHY DO YOU ALWAYS HAVE TO TALK TO THEM FIRST?
SHUT UP, IT'S NOT EVERY DAY YOU GET TO MEET YOUR HEROES.
PLEASE DON'T!!

SHHHHHHH.
WE'RE TRYING TO BE COVERT AND SHIT.
MMMM!!
MMMM
MMMPPPFFF
TEXT THEM AND LET THEM KNOW IT'S DONE.
WANNA GET SOMETHING TO EAT?
I DON'T EAT AFTER 7 PM.
UGH, FOR CHRIST'S SAKE.

Kay Cee
It's done
HEY, THUNDER.
IT'S DONE.
GOOD. WHAT'S THE STATUS ON JOE DOAKES?
HIS LAST MESSAGE SAID HE WAS FOLLOWING JACK HAMMER AND A WOMAN.
I HAVEN'T HEARD FROM HIM SINCE.
SHOULD I SEND SOMEONE TO FIND HIM?
NO. I'M SURE HE'LL CHECK IN.
FOR NOW, LET'S BRING A LITTLE THUNDER DOWN ON THE PRESS.
WWFX.COM

CRASH
EVERYBODY FRONT AND CENTER!! GET YOUR ASSES OUT HERE!!
WELL, WELL, WELL. YOU PEOPLE HAVE BEEN BUSY.
YOU KNOW YOU SHOULD STICK TO STORIES ABOUT NATIONAL CAT DAY.
BECAUSE IF YOU KEEP POKING YOUR NOISES INTO MY AFFAIRS...
SOMEONE COULD GET HURT.
NOW. WHO WROTE THAT STORY ABOUT ME?
IT WAS ME!

HAVE THOSE NUT HUGGERS YOU'RE WEARING CUT THE FLOW OF BLOOD TO YOUR BRAIN? YOU CAN'T JUST COME IN HERE BREAKING SHIT!
FREEDOM OF THE PRESS, ASSHOLES. THE VERY THING YOU MUSCLE HEADS ARE SUPPOSED TO PROTECT!!
GARRH!
BOOM
NOW GET THE FUCK OUT BEFORE I CALL THE COPS!
OK. YOU'VE MADE YOUR DECISION.
SMACK
THAT CRAP CAUSES BLOATING.

YOU DIDN'T HAVE TO DO THAT, PECKS. BUT THANKS.
HEY, WE WROTE THAT STORY TOGETHER. AND WE'RE GOING TO FINISH IT AND EXPOSE THUNDER FOR THE LYING PSYCHOPATH HE REALLY IS.
YOU GOTTA BE CAREFUL. MORE IMPORTANT PEOPLE THAN US HAVE DISAPPEARED GETTING IN THE WAY OF MEN LIKE THUNDER.
UGH.
WE'LL BE FINE. I'M GOING HOME TO SOAK IN SOME EPSOM SALT. THAT DESK WAS HEAVY.
OK. GOODNIGHT.
WWF
I'LL GIVE YOU A FIGHTING CHANCE.

THAT'S HONORABLE!
BUT STUPID!
HUUHH!!
YEAH! THAT'S IT.
WANT SOME MORE, YOU SICK FUCK?!
CRACK
AHHHHHH!!!
HA! GOOD MATCH--BUT IT'S OVER NOW.

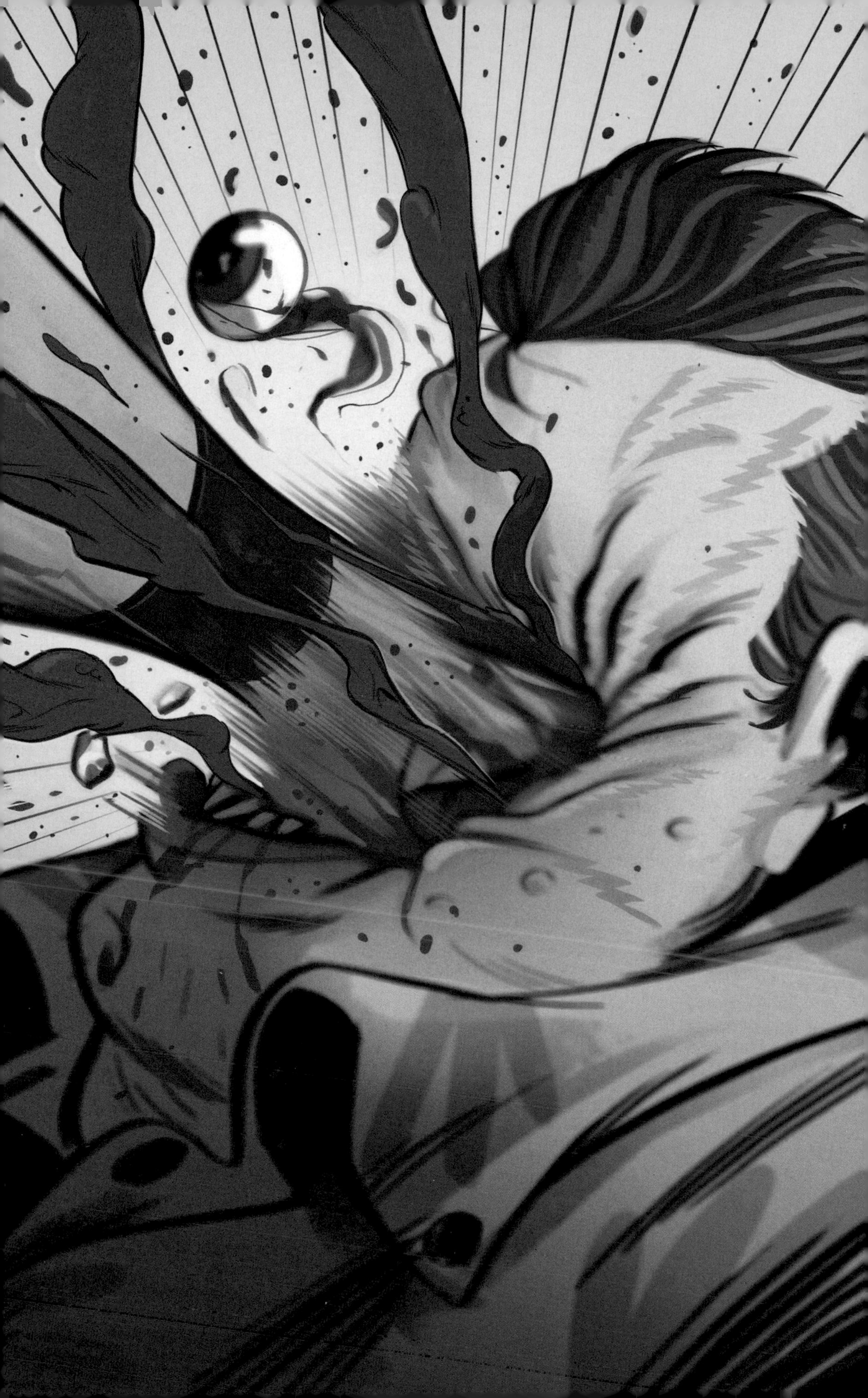

MMMMUUUFF!!
CLICK
WOOP WOOOP
CLANK
SLLLING!
GLUUSHH!!!
YOU FOUGHT WELL. YOU'LL MAKE A FINE TROPHY.
WE NEED TO GO, AND THERE'S STILL NO WORD FROM--

"--JOE DOAKES."
COME ON YOU SON OF A--
CLINK
NOW FOR A LITTLE PICK-ME-UP.
EENY. MEENY. MINY.
MOE!!
AHHHHRRR!!

WE HAVE A FEW QUESTIONS.

ROUND
2

ALTERNATE COVER BY SANFORD GREEN

NIXX ENTERPRISES.
BLUE DIARRHEA.
WHAT?
I SAID, "BLUE DIARRHEA." NIXX CAUSES IT.
IT WASN'T EASY GETTING YOU INVITED TO THIS MEETING, BIG GAME. DON'T EMBARRASS ME.
NIXX MAKES THESE LITTLE BLUE SNACK CAKES.
PEOPLE EAT THAT SHIT AND--
BOOM!
EXPLOSIVE, BLUE-COLORED DIARRHEA FOR DAYS!
WHAT WAS THE NAME OF THOSE CAKES?
CRAZY CAKES?
FLAKY CAKES?

FROSTY CAKES.
YEAH, THAT'S IT!
ding
I DON'T TRUST THESE PEOPLE, THUNDER.
JUST RELAX, THEY'RE USEFUL-- FOR NOW.
FOR CHRIST'S SAKE! WHY ARE YOU STILL WEARING THAT, CHARLES?!
CHARLES ISN'T MY TRUE NAME. I AM THE THUNDER BEAR--
CUT THE SHIT, YOU AND CONGRESS CAN PRANCE AROUND FOR THE CAMERAS WEARING THAT FAGGOTY SHIT! BUT YOU PUT ON A GODDAMN TIE IN MY PRESENCE!

THESE PERSONAS THE MEN AND WOMEN OF CONGRESS HAVE TAKEN MEAN SOMETHING.
PLEASE SHOW SOME RESPECT.
YEAH, WHATEVER. I ASKED YOU HERE FOR AN UPDATE ON THE MUTANT UPGRADE BILL. THE MUTANT LUCHADORS HAVE TEETH AND CLAWS!
THE BACK ALLEY FIGHTS IN MEXICO GET MILLIONS OF VIEWS. THE MUTANTS IN CONGRESS NEED THOSE UPGRADES.
WE NEED YOU AND BIG GAME TO GET THE RESTRICTIONS ON MUTANT GENETIC ENHANCEMENT LIFTED.
REVENUE IN ADVERTISING AND STUMP PRODUCTION ALONE WOULD BE IN THE BILLIONS.
BUT WHAT ABOUT THE SLAY ACT?! I'VE SET THINGS IN MOTION THAT CAN GET THE BILL PASSED!

FORGET IT. WE'RE BACKING THE FREAKS.

FORGET IT?! WE'VE BEEN WORKING ON THIS PLAN FOR MORE THAN A YEAR. THIS ISN'T ABOUT A REVENUE STREAM.

IT'S ABOUT PRIMAL POWER, FAITH, AND COUNTRY!

NOW, YOU'RE GONNA CONTINUE TO FUND THE SLAY ACT, OR I'M GONNA BREAK YOUR GODDAMN JAW.

YOU KNOW, MY CONSTITUENTS NAMED THIS ***THE VICE GRIP*** WHEN I WAS IN CONGRESS.

I USED TO BE ABLE TO CHOKE A MAN WITHIN AN INCH OF HIS LIFE.
FOCUS ON THE MUTANTS OR THE MONEY DRIES UP. PERIOD.
GAAAKKK!
UHHHH...
AND CLEAN THAT UP.

ding
ding
=SIGH=
ding
TODAY
Where R U?
Y?
What do U mean Y???
I'm working
I need you home.
For What?? I'm busy.
Just forget it. BYE.
Type a message
FOR FUCK'S SAKE.
=GASP=
AHHHHHRRAA!

JACK!!!

GIVE ME THAT! ARE YOU TRYING TO KILL 'IM?!
IT'S A MIRACLE HE HASN'T PASSED OUT!
I NEED TO QUESTION HIM!
HEY! YOU ASKED FOR MY HELP, SO I'M HELPING!
KRAK
KRAK! KRAK! KRAK!
HEADS UP, BUTTHOLES.

KRRRAACKKK
DAMN IT!
GET BACK HERE!
HA! NO THANKS!
KILL YA LATER!

I'M GONNA NEED YOU TO LET THIS GO, ABE.
CAN YOU BE MORE SPECIFIC? I'VE GOT A LOT OF PROJECTS ON MY PLATE, JOSH.
THE SLAY ACT, DAMN IT!
STOP POSTING "ANONYMOUS" ARTICLES THAT COULD GET US ALL KILLED.
PECKS AND I ARE ON TO SOMETHING BIG. WHY DO YOU THINK THUNDER AND GAME CAME HERE WITH THAT *SOPRANOS* TOUGH-GUY BULLSHIT?

PECKS IS DEAD.
THERE'S NO BODY. NO MISSING PERSONS REPORT WILL BE FILED. NO DETECTIVE IS GOING TO LOOK INTO THIS. BUT YOU KNOW HE'S DEAD, ABE.
THUNDER DOESN'T GIVE A SHIT. HE DOES WHAT HE WANTS TO WHOM HE WANTS. AND OUR LITTLE NEWSFEED IS IN HIS CROSSHAIRS BECAUSE OF YOU.
I HAVE KIDS. A WIFE. PLEASE JUST STOP, OR YOU'RE FIRED.
HEY, JOHNNIE. YEAH, IT'S BEEN A LONG TIME. YOU STILL HAVE THAT ANTIQUE BOOK FOR SALE?
YEAH, I KNOW THE PRICE.
I'M WILLING TO PAY IT.

JACK, ARE YOU CONSCIOUS?
I WISH I WASN'T. THIS HURTS.
IT'S GONNA TAKE THE BOTH OF US TO LIFT THIS THING.
LIFT ON THE COUNT OF THREE.
WAIT. LIFT ON THREE, OR AFTER WE SAY THREE?
THIS ISN'T THE TIME TO BE AN ASSHOLE!
ONE... TWO...
RAAHHHH!

A CONCUSSION, CONTUSIONS, AND A CHIPPED TOOTH, BUT NO ANSWERS.
I DIDN'T TELL YOU I WAS MARRIED.
YOU SHOULD CALL YOUR HUSBAND, HAVE HIM TAKE YOU TO A HOSPITAL.
YOU DIDN'T HAVE TO. SOMEBODY'S BEEN BLOWING UP YOUR PHONE SINCE WE MET.
MIND YOUR OWN GODDAMN BUSINESS, JACK. I NEED TO GET THUNDER. I NEED TO FINISH THIS.
I MAY KNOW SOME PEOPLE THAT CAN HELP.
GIVE ME YOUR PHONE.
SHIT!
FUCK IT!!!
LISTEN. WE'RE GONNA GET THUNDER. BECAUSE OF HIM, SOMEONE TRIED TO KILL ME, SOMEONE STABBED ME, AND A BUILDING FELL ON US.
I'M GONNA SHOVE THAT SLAY ACT RIGHT UP HIS ASS.
WE DON'T NEED THE PHONE. WE'LL JUST DROP IN ON MY FRIENDS.

"YOU EVER HEAR OF THE BLACKSMITHS?"
VIRGINIA.
SO WHAT'D THEY DO?
DOES IT MATTER?
WE WERE PROTESTING! PEACEFULLY!
YOU HAVE NO RIGHT TO DETAIN US!
DON'T WORRY, WE'LL LET YOU GO WHEN WE'RE... DONE.
WHAT THE HELL HAPPENED TO THE LIGHTS?

AHHH!
UHHGG!
CRACK!!!
WHO IS SHE?
JUST RUN!

WHAT DO YOU KNOW ABOUT THE BLACKSMITHS? MOST PEOPLE DON'T EVEN THINK THEY'RE REAL.
COME ON, STOP PRETENDING THE FBI DOESN'T HAVE A FILE ON THEM.
WE DO, BUT IT'S A VERY SMALL FILE.
THEY POPPED UP AROUND 1866. THEY TAUGHT FORMER SLAVES TO READ, WRITE, AND FIGHT.
NOW, THEY BREAK THE LAW AND TEACH MINORITIES WITHOUT A LITERACY LICENSE TO READ.
PRETTY GOOD INTEL. BUT THEY WERE FORMED IN 1863, NOT '66. AND TODAY'S LITERACY LAWS ARE ACTUALLY BASED ON INCOME LEVEL. SO, THE BLACKSMITHS WILL TEACH ANYONE, NOT JUST MINORITIES.
BUT WHY ARE WE AT THE CAPITOL?
THIS BUILDING WAS BUILT BY SLAVES WHO WOULD BECOME THE FIRST BLACKSMITHS IN 1863.

THE ORIGINAL HEADQUARTERS IS HIDDEN BENEATH THE CAPITOL.
I DON'T SEE ANYTHING.
LOOK CLOSER.
YOU SON OF A--!
AHHHHHHHH!
HEY, JACK!
WHAT'S UP, HAMZA?
GABRIEL DOESN'T WANT TO SEE YOU! HE'S PISSED!
YEAH, WELL, HE'S ALWAYS PISSED. AND DON'T SAY **PISSED!**
THIS TECHNOLOGY IS **FORBIDDEN.** NO ONE'S SUPPOSED TO EVEN KNOW IT EXISTS.
YEAH, I KNOW, A LOT OF STUFF IS FORBIDDEN HERE.
WELCOME TO--

--the FORGE!
JACK HAMMER?! WHATEVER TROUBLE YOU'RE IN, TAKE IT AWAY FROM ME AND MY BLACKSMITHS!

ONCE THUNDER GETS THE SANCTIONS LIFTED ON GENETIC ENHANCEMENTS, EVERY DAY IS GONNA BE LIKE CHRISTMAS MORNING.
USING MORE AGGRESSIVE MUTANTS ON THE STUMP IS JUST THE BEGINNING. WE CAN SELL ENHANCEMENTS AS DESIGNER DRUGS, OR TO ATHLETES, THE GOVERNMENT. JUST IMAGINE WHAT THESE ENHANCEMENTS WILL DO IN THE HANDS OF THE RIGHT ASSASSIN.
UGGGGHH!
WHAT THE HELL?!

I'LL SHOW YA WHAT THE UPGRADES CAN DO!
CHUNK
SQUISHHHH
SLASHHHH

HELLO, MR. HAIL!
I HAVE RESOURCES YOU CAN'T EVEN IMAGINE. JUST NAME A NUMBER, PLACE, OR PERSON AND IT'S YOURS.
OUR MISSION IS DONE, HAIL. THERE'S NO NEED TO BARGAIN.
YEAH, BABY, YOU CAN'T TALK YOUR WAY OUT OF THIS ONE.
DON'T BE SCARED. YOU'RE NOT GONNA DIE. WE'RE JUST HERE TO DELIVER THE MESSAGE THAT YOU FUCKED WITH THE WRONG GUY.
POOP!
THE CLIENT WANTS YOU ALLLL TO HIMSELF.

ROUND 3

Thirty-Eighth Congress of the United States of America;

At the second Session,

Begun and held at the City of Washington, on Monday, the fifth day of December, one thousand eight hundred and sixty-four.

A RESOLUTION

Submitting to the legislatures of the several States a proposition to amend the Constitution of the United States.

Resolved by the Senate and House of Representatives of the United States of America in Congress assembled,

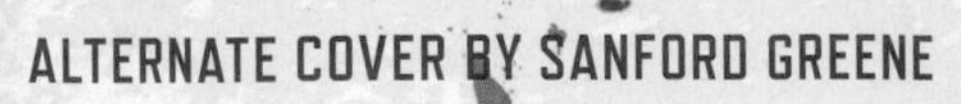

ALTERNATE COVER BY SANFORD GREENE

GET OUT, JACK!
GET OUT AND DON'T GET THIS YOUNG WOMAN INVOLVED IN YOUR SHENANIGANS.
FIRST OF ALL, SHE DRAGGED ME INTO HER SHENANIGANS.
AND SECOND, I THINK IT'S FUCKING HILARIOUS YOU USED SHENANIGANS IN A SENTENCE.
STOP CURSING!
GABRIEL, I'M SPECIAL AGENT ANNABELLE LISTER. JACK AND I ARE ON A MISSION TO STOP CONGRESSMAN THUNDER BEARER. HE'S TRYING TO PASS--
THE SLAY ACT. YES. I KNOW.

SO, YOU'RE ALREADY WORKING ON THIS? WHAT INTEL HAVE YOU GATHERED? HOW MANY BLACKSMITHS DO YOU HAVE DEDICATED TO THE MISSION?
ZERO.
WHAT DO YOU MEAN ZERO?
I'M AWARE OF WHAT THUNDER BEARER IS UP TO. FRANKLY, IT DOESN'T CONCERN THE BLACKSMITHS.
COME ON, GABRIEL! JUST GIVE US A FEW SOLDIERS AND SOME INTEL. ANYTHING.
YOU PEOPLE BREAK EVERY DAMN LAW IN THE BOOK. BUT WHEN YOU HAVE A CHANCE TO BRING DOWN A LUNATIC THAT WRITES SHITTY POLICY JUST ABOVE YOU, YOU DO NOTHING?!
MRS. LISTER, I HAD YOUR FILE PULLED AS SOON YOU SET FOOT ON THE CAPITOL STEPS. YOU HAVE NO RIGHT TO LECTURE ME.
YOU'VE BEEN SUSPENDED FROM THE FBI FOR 6 MONTHS ON PSYCH LEAVE, AND HAVE KNOWINGLY WORKED FOR AN ORGANIZATION THAT ENFORCES THE LAWS THAT KEEP YOUR OWN PEOPLE OPPRESSED.

SUSPENDED? YOU SAID YOU WERE ON LEAVE. ARE YOU FUCKING SERIOUS?! THIS IS WHY YOU HAVEN'T CALLED FOR BACKUP?
CALM DOWN, JACK. WE CAN DO THIS WITHOUT THE FBI. THUNDER HAD SOMEBODY ON THE INSIDE AND HE GOT ME FIRED. THE PSYCH EVALUATION WAS BULLSHIT!
WHAT AM I EVEN DOING HERE? I'LL GET PAYBACK ON MY OWN.
THIS IS BIGGER THAN PAYBACK, THE BLACKSMITHS' SECRETS, OR MY JOB.
THINGS ARE BAD NOW BUT THEY'RE ABOUT TO GET WORSE!
LET HIM GO. HE'S NOT THE HERO YOU THINK HE IS.
WE HAVE TO DO SOMETHING.
THERE'S NOTHING WE CAN DO FOR YOU, DEAR.
OF COURSE THERE IS.

I COULDN'T HELP OVERHEARING ALL THE SCREAMING IN OUR SUPER-SECRET LOCATION.
THUNDER IS A NOTORIOUS TECHNOPHOBE. HE HAS HARD COPIES OF ALL HIS DEALINGS IN A BUILDING ONLY A FEW MILES FROM HERE.
I BET THE H.N.I.C DIDN'T TELL YOU THAT.
STAND DOWN, NATHALIE.
MY FRIENDS CALL ME NAT.
ANNA.
THE DOCUMENTS ARE IN A LOCKED OFFICE AND THE BUILDING IS WELL PROTECTED.
WE CAN GO OVER A PLAN, GRAB SOME WEAPONS, AND HIT IT WHEN IT GETS DARK.
NO, NATHALIE. I SAID **STAND DOWN.**
WHAT'S THE POINT OF ALL THIS TRAINING AND KNOWLEDGE IF WE DON'T USE IT TO DO THINGS THAT **MATTER?!**
WE'RE GOING!
BYE, GABE.
DO YOU WANT ME TO FOLLOW THEM?
SIGH
TWO WARS, 18 RACE RIOTS, AND ONE ASSASSINATION ATTEMPT. AND THAT CHILD IS GOING TO BE WHAT KILLS ME.
YES, FOLLOW THEM.

HOT DOG
I'M GONNA HAVE A LIGHT SNACK THEN FIND THAT DAMN CLOWN.
BIGGER THAN PAYBACK... AIN'T NOTHING BIGGER THAN THAT.
DAMN RIGHT.
SHIT.
CAN I FINISH MY HOT DOGS FIRST?

UMPH!!
HOT DOG
I'M A FAN, JACK.
I USED TO WATCH YOU AND THE OTHER FIGHTERS ON THE INTERNET WHEN I WAS IN THE REEDUCATION CAMPS. I THOUGHT YOU GUYS WERE GODS.
SORRY YOU DIDN'T HAVE BETTER ROLE MODELS, KID.
I USE TO FIGHT TO BAN THOSE CAMPS.

I KNOW.
NOW YOU FIGHT ALONGSIDE THE FBI. THE SAME MOTHERFUCKERS THAT DRAGGED ME AND MY BOYFRIEND INTO THE STREET. THEY PUT A CLUSTER OF BULLETS IN HIS CHEST.
THEN THEY LOCKED ME AWAY AND TURNED ME INTO THIS.
TECHNICALLY, ANNA WAS FIRED FROM THE FBI.
NOW, ARE YOU GONNA TAKE ME TO YOUR BOSS OR TALK SHIT ALL DAY?
THUNDER SAID I COULD MOVE OUT OF CLOWN CLASS IF I BROUGHT YOU IN, JACK.
OHHH, WHAT A HAPPY DAY!
UM, GOOD.
POW!!

MADAM MAYHEM
WHERE ARE YA, BOBBY? I'M HERE TO RELIEVE YOU.
BOBBY?!
HURRY UP BEFORE THE BITCH SCREAMS.

I GOT 'IM. JUST GET US INSIDE.

THE DOCUMENTS ARE IN AN OFFICE. SHOULD BE IN THE BACK. WE JUST NEED TO FIND IT AND--
WAIT. ALL OF THE CUSTOMERS IN HERE ARE SENATORS.
YEAH, THAT'S NO SURPRISE. THEY'RE ALL PROBABLY BOUGHT AND PAID FOR BY THE SAME PEOPLE THAT OWN THUNDER AND PUSH THE SLAY ACT.
RIGHT, BUT DID YOUR INTEL SAY ANYTHING ABOUT *THIS?*
OH! NO, THE DRUG-FUELED ORGY IS NEW. LET'S HURRY BEFORE THEY COME DOWN AND WE GET CAUGHT.

MARYLAND.
THUNDER BEARER!! I'M GONNA KILL YOU--
WHAT IS THIS SHIT?

YOU SICK SON OF A BITCH.
SWOOSHHH
CLAMP
PECKS WAS A FIGHTER-- A REAL WARRIOR. HE DIED ON HIS FEET.
BUT YOU'RE GONNA FUCKING KNEEL!

CRACK!
ALRIGHT! STOP! YOU'LL HAVE MY FULL SUPPORT ON THE SLAY ACT. JUST GET THIS GODDAMN THING OFF OF ME.
THIS ISN'T JUST ABOUT THE SLAY ACT. IT'S ABOUT LIFE AND DEATH.
I GIVE PRAISE TO THE ONE TRUE WAY OF LIFE. THE WAY OF WAR AND COMBAT, OF THE BEGINNING, THE END, AND REBIRTH.
PECKS WILL LIVE ON AS A TRIBUTE TO OUR MATCH.
I'M FEEDING YOUR HEAD TO MY DOGS!
SLING!
AAAK

IT'S BEEN A LONG TIME SINCE I HAD SOMEONE TO OPEN YOU.
SPEAK TO ME.
TIC
TIC
TIC
TIC
CLICK

PLEASE, HURRY AND FIND SOMETHING. SHIT'S GETTING REALLY WEIRD OUT THERE.
THERE'S A TON OF FILES HERE. I'M GONNA NEED MORE TIME.
THK
THK
THK
TIME'S UP!
YOU SNEAK INTO MY PLACE AND GO THROUGH MY SHIT?!
DON'T BOTHER TELLING ME WHO YOU ARE. I'LL KNOW EVERYTHING AFTER I'M DONE.

YOU BITCHES ARE GONNA NEED A SAFE WORD!
ARE YOU FBI? DCPD? YOU'RE NOT GONNA TAKE THIS PLACE AWAY FROM ME!
EVERY BRICK, CHAIR, WALL, WET PUSSY, AND DICK BELONGS TO ME!

IT'S MINE!!

HEY, ANNA! LITTLE HELP OVER HERE?!
THERE WAS SOMETHING ON THE TIP OF THE DARTS. I CAN'T FEEL MY ARM!
YOU'VE GOT TWO ARMS!
URGH!
CRASH!

UHHH...IF WE'RE GONNA FIGHT, YOU GUYS HAVE TO PUT SOME CLOTHES ON.
I AGREE.
IT SMELLS LIKE CHEAP GIN AND UNWASHED DICKS IN HERE.
HEY, JACK. MEET NAT. NAT, THIS IS JACK.
HEY.
AHH, COOL. I'VE BEEN STUCK WITH THIS CLOWN ALL DAY.
HEY, WE JUST FOUGHT A DOMINATRIX.
SHUT THE FUCK UP!
SAVE YA VOICES FOR ALL THE PLEADING AND SCREAMING.

IN THE BEGINNING, THERE WAS PEACE. THE UNIVERSE WAS TRILLIONS OF YEARS OLD AND ONLY BEASTS AND WILD THINGS ROAMED THE PLANETS.
THEN GOD CLENCHED HIS FIST AND STRUCK DOWN THE SAVAGE LAND AND OUR WORLD WAS BORN OUT OF PURE DESTRUCTIVE POWER.
=SIGH=

10.
9. 8. 7. 6.
5. 4.
CLICK
CLICK
3. 2.
1!!
CLICK
CLICK

TIC
CLICK
TIC
CLICK
TIC
CLICK
TIC
TIC
TIC
CLICK
ONLY THE BELIEVER THAT EMBRACES DEATH SHALL LOOK UPON MY WORDS. READ MY CREED AND WEEP WITH JOY.
USE THESE PAGES AND ACT NOW AND SLAY THE UNWORTHY IN THE NAME OF MIGHT, WAR, AND DEATH.

ROUND 4

ALTERNATE COVER BY SANFORD GREENE

WE'RE NOT DOING THAT.
MADAMA MAYEM
WHY WOULD ANYONE DO THAT?!
COME ON, WHY NOT?
BECAUSE IT'S STUPID AND GROSS. NOW GET THUNDER ON THE PHONE!
Thunder

VERY NICE.
buzz buzzzz

WHAT IS IT?
WE HAVE JACK AND HIS FRIENDS HERE AT MAYHEM'S CLUB.
SHOW ME.
IS THAT FORMER AGENT LISTER? I HAD BRUNCH WITH YOUR COMMANDING OFFICER A FEW DAYS AGO. HE REALLY MISSES YOU.
TALK SHIT WHILE YOU CAN, THUNDER.
JACK HAMMER, YOU'VE BEEN HALF DEAD FOR YEARS. YOU SHOULD HAVE JUST LET SWEET SMELL FINISH THE JOB.
NOW YOU'RE HELPING THE FBI? SINCE YOU SURVIVED I WAS GOING TO GIVE YOU A JOB, BUT NOW I GOTTA KILL YOU.

YOU STARTED THIS, THUNDER. I TOOK SWEET SMELL'S MONEY TO THROW THE FIGHT, BUT YOU WANTED HIM TO KILL ME OVER A STUPID PIECE OF LEGISLATION.
THERE'S WAR SOUTH OF THE BORDER. FAMINE AND DROUGHT IN CALIFORNIA AND 80 PERCENT OF AMERICANS LIVE IN POVERTY. THEY NEED US AND THE FIGHTS TO DISTRACT THEM.
SO WHEN NIXX INDUSTRIES ASKED ME TO FIND A WAY TO INCREASE RATINGS--I SUGGESTED THE SLAY ACT.
BUT IT'S NOT JUST A PIECE OF LEGISLATION. IT DATES BACK TO--
Messages
STOP.
I DON'T GIVE A DAMN ABOUT WHAT YOU'RE DOING OR WHY. I'M GONNA RUIN YOU THEN BEAT THE SHIT OUTTA YOU.
I HAVEN'T SEEN FIRE LIKE THIS FROM YOU IN YEARS, JACK! YOU KNOW YOU WERE MY FIRST PROFESSIONAL STUMP FIGHT. YOU WERE MY FUCKING IDOL! I DIDN'T WANT TO JUST KILL YOU, JACK. I WANTED TO MAKE YOU IMMORTAL. YOU WERE TO BE MY SACRIFICE TO THE GODS. I WAS GOING TO GIVE YOU THE HONOR OF USHERING IN THE DEATH OF THE OLD WORLD AND THE BIRTH OF A NEW ONE.
YOU'RE A FUCKING LOON. ARE WE DONE YET?
YEAH, WE'RE DONE. BRING ME THEIR HEADS, JOE, AND YOU'LL BE FREE FROM THE PROGRAM.

WILL DO.
I'M NOT DYING IN A FREAKING STRIP CLUB.
NAT, DO YOU THINK YOUR DAD HAD SOMEONE FOLLOW YOU?
OF COURSE HE HAD SOMEONE FOLLOW ME.
KLANK
WHOOSSH
KLANK
WHOOS

DOAKES! WHAT'S HAPPENING?
I'LL TAKE THAT.
THUNDER BEARER, THIS IS GABRIEL, THE LEADER OF THE D.C. BLACKSMITHS.
BLACKSMITHS?!? THERE'S NO SUCH THING! JUST BEDTIME STORIES FOR BLACK PEOPLE.
WE'RE VERY REAL AND SO ARE MY CONNECTIONS. THE FBI ARE ON THEIR WAY TO ARREST THIS CULT YOU'VE BUILT FOR ATTEMPTED MURDER. AND IT WON'T BE LONG BEFORE IT ALL LEADS BACK TO YOU.
IF YOU REALLY ARE THE BLACKSMITHS I'M GONNA **FIND** YOU!
IF IT MEANS PROTECTING THE FUTURE FROM YOU THAT'S A RISK I'M WILLING TO TAKE.
HEY, THUNDER. I'M GONNA TAKE A SHOWER, GET BANDAGED UP, THEN I'M COMING TO WHUP YOUR ASS BEFORE YOU GO TO JAIL!

CRACK
CRUNCH
YOLANDA! I NEED CAM AND KAY CEE.
I'VE ALREADY TRIED BUT THEY'RE UNAVAILABLE.
JUST GET ME SOMEBODY TO KILL THEM!
WHAT ARE YOU GOING TO DO ABOUT THE CONSTRUCTION, THE SLAY ACT, AND JACK HAMMER?
I-- I DON'T KNOW.
I THINK I MAY HAVE FOUND SOMETHING THAT WILL SPARK SOME IDEAS.

I'LL HAVE CONSTRUCTION DONE BY THE END OF TODAY.
AND I'LL HAVE THE TECH GUYS SET UP A BROADCAST FOR TOMORROW. I HAVE SOMETHING TO SAY TO JACK HAMMER.
GOOD BOY.

THIS ISN'T SUPPOSED TO BE HERE.
GHRRRRRRRR
THE REPTILE-BASED SENATORS SHOULD BE BARREN LIKE ALL MUTANTS.
BEING STERILE IS BUILT INTO THE MUTANTS' GENETIC CODE. I DON'T KNOW IF I SHOULD CALL THIS THING A MIRACLE OR AN ABOMINATION.
IT'S BEAUTIFUL.
BEAUTIFUL? ARE YOU KIDDING?
ding ding
UH-- GIVE ME A SEC.
Abe
I need you to come over
911
Type a message

HEY, SHANNON, LET'S FIGURE THIS OUT TOMORROW. I HAVE A FAMILY THING I NEED TO TAKE CARE OF.
SURE, NICK. SEE YOU TOMORROW.
CLICK
AND THE BEASTS SHALL ROAM THE EARTH AGAIN.

THE FORGE.
I DON'T WANT TO BE A WET BLANKET, BUT THUNDER OWNS THE FBI AND THE D.C. POLICE. HOW IS THIS GONNA STICK?
DON'T WORRY. IT'S LIKE MY DAD SAID. HE HAS CONNECTIONS.
THAT A BADGE? YOU CAN'T BE SERIOUS?
DOESN'T MATTER WHAT TEAM I FIGHT WITH. IT'S THE CAUSE THAT MATTERS.
AHHHH, THAT'S BEAUTIFUL.
SHUT UP.
NAT, RALLY AS MANY OF YOUR OFFICERS AS YOU CAN. ANNA, REACH OUT TO ANY AGENT THAT WILL LISTEN AND CONVINCE THEM TO ISSUE A WARRANT FOR THUNDER'S ARREST.
I'M SURE HE'LL PUT UP A FIGHT.
BA-DOO

URRHG!
OH, YES! IT IS GOING TO BE ONE HELL OF A FIGHT!

TAKE 'EM DOWN!

BLAAAA URRRRRGGGGGG AHHHH!!!
URRRRGH
COUGH COUGH!
UNCLE ABE, IS THAT YOU?!?
JESUS CHRIST, WHAT HAPPENED?
COME ON, I'LL CALL AN AMBULANCE.
NO, JUST HELP ME BACK TO MY DESK.

WOW, I REALLY DO HAVE A LOT OF COOL SHIT.
YEAH-- I GUESS.
WE NEED TO GET YOU TO A DOCTOR, UNCLE ABE.
NICK--HISTORY AND THE HUMANITIES ARE SLOWLY BECOMING EXTINCT FROM HIGH SCHOOL AND COLLEGE CAMPUSES.
YOU HAVE, LIKE, TWO PHDS BUT HAVE YOU EVER SAT THROUGH A HISTORY LECTURE?
WELL, NO, CAN'T SAY I EVER HAVE.
THEN LET ME GIVE YOU A CRASH COURSE ABOUT FIGHTING ON THE STUMP.

"A LONG TIME AGO DELEGATES USED TO DEBATE ON STUMPS, NOT FIGHT ON THEM.
"THEY WERE NOT CIVILIZED BY ANY MEANS BUT IT WASN'T THE MADNESS WE HAVE TODAY.
"IT ALL STARTED IN 1868 WHEN PRESIDENTIAL CANDIDATE HORATIO SEYMOUR LOST HIS TEMPER AT A DEBATE AND NEARLY BEAT ULYSSES S. GRANT TO DEATH.
"WORD OF THE FIGHT SPREAD AND SEYMOUR'S POPULARITY SOARED. EVERYONE WAS CAUGHT UP IN IT. CITIZENS, CONGRESSIONAL RECONSTRUCTION, THE WORLD, EVERYONE! AND STUMP FIGHTING WAS BORN.
"BUT WHAT THE NATION DIDN'T KNOW WAS THAT BEYOND THE STUMP AND POLITICS THERE EXISTED A CHURCH OF DEATH AND WAR. SENATOR THUNDER BEARER AND HIS DISCIPLES STILL PRACTICE THE RELIGION."

SITTING ON MY DESK IS THEIR BIBLE.
I BELIEVE THUNDER IS USING IT AS A ROAD MAP TO DO SOMETHING HORRIBLE. I NEED YOU TO CONTINUE MY RESEARCH, NICK, AND STOP HIM.
I'VE DIGITIZED THE BOOK FOR YOU. READING THE HARD COPY WILL KILL YOU SO NEVER TRY TO OPEN IT. I WAS IN CONTACT WITH AN FBI AGENT NAMED ANNA LISTER. SHE CAN HELP YOU.
WHOA WHOA! THIS IS TOO MUCH INFO TOO FAST. START FROM THE BEGINNING. WHERE DID YOU GET THE BOOK?!
GULP GULP
BLAAAA URRRRRRGGGGGG AHHHH!!!

ROUND
5

ALTERNATE COVER BY SANFORD GREENE

20 YEARS AGO.
GALACTIC COMICS
JACK HAMMER, THE NEW SC SENATOR, IS FIGHTING TO BRING AWARENESS TO--AND ABOLISH--BLACK CODES ACROSS THE NATION!
THE YOUNG THUNDER BEARER IS RUNNING FOR THE CALIFORNIA SENATE. HE'S HERE TO SHOW THE VOTERS WHAT HE'S GOT, AND THE HAMMER WAS KIND ENOUGH TO GIVE HIM A BOUT!
OOOH! THE HAMMER EXPLODES INTO ACTION!
IT'S BEEN OVER AN HOUR, BUT IT'S FINALLY OVER!

THAT WAS AN AMAZING FIGHT, FOLKS! JACK HAMMER HAS WON THE DAY, BUT THIS WON'T BE THE LAST TIME YOU HEAR THE NAME THUNDER BEARER!
GALACTIC COMICZ
MOVE! OUT OF THE WAY!
SENIOR SENATOR SWAN PSALMS! I DIDN'T KNOW YOU WERE HERE, DID YOU CATCH THE MATCH?
JACK, YOU NEED TO GO HOME RIGHT AWAY!
WHAT ARE YOU TALKING ABOUT, MIMMS?
GALACTIC COMICZ
IT'S YOUR WIFE!

POLICE
911
JANIE! WHERE ARE YOU?!
SHE'S OVER HERE, MR. HAMMOND.
YOUR WIFE HAS ILLEGALLY OBTAINED HER LITERACY LICENSE AND THAT'S A FEDERAL CRIME.
YOU OK, JANIE?
WHAT'S THIS **REALLY** ABOUT!?

YOU WANT TO CHANGE THE WORLD. MAKE IT A BETTER PLACE. BUT THE WORLD DOESN'T BELONG TO YOU. AND YOU PISSED OFF THE PEOPLE WHO ACTUALLY RUN SHIT.
CONSIDER THIS A WARNING. JUST REMEMBER TO PLAY NICE AND EVERYTHING WILL BE FINE.
EVERYBODY OUT!
LET'S LEAVE SO THESE FOLKS CAN ENJOY THE REST OF THEIR DAY.
WHO THE HELL ARE YOU?
YOLANDA YANKS, THE PERSON ALLOWING YOUR FAMILY TO LIVE.
OUR CHILD WILL NEVER BE SAFE. I HAVE TO DISAPPEAR.
I KNOW.

THESE THINGS LOOK LIKE THEY WERE CREATED IN A LAB! I GUESS THUNDER'S STOPPED PULLING PUNCHES...
ZZSHSHZZSHSH
HEY, GUYS? SOMETHING'S HAPPENING...

HELLO, WORLD.
I'D LIKE TO INVITE YOU TO WITNESS THE FIRST OFFICIAL DEATH MATCH ON THE STUMP. I PROMISE YOU THE MOST EPIC BATTLE YOU'VE EVER SEEN. BETWEEN MYSELF AND--
--SENATOR JACK HAMMER.
AND JACK, IF YOU DON'T SHOW, I'LL BROADCAST THE NAME AND LOCATION OF YOUR WIFE AND CHILD. EVERY ENEMY YOU'VE EVER MADE, INCLUDING MYSELF, WILL SHOW UP AT THEIR DOORSTEP.
IT'S THE SLAY ACT SHOWDOWN, AMERICA. NOON TOMORROW ON THE NIXX INDUSTRIES ROOFTOP. LIVE.
HE'S LOST IT, JACK. HE WANTS YOU TO DIE IN THAT RING.
I KNOW. BUT I GOTTA GO.
I NEED TO STAY HERE TO HELP THE BLACKSMITHS. THEY NEED TO RELOCATE AND DO SOME DAMAGE CONTROL, NOW THAT THE WORLD KNOWS THEY EXIST. BESIDES, I'M DONE LETTING PEOPLE LIKE THUNDER DICTATE MY LIFE.
YOU CAN TAKE IT FROM HERE.
SEE YOU AROUND, ANNA.

REST WELL, ABRAHAM. YOUR WORK IS DONE.
NICHOLAS!
SHOW SOME RESPECT FOR THE DEAD, CHILD!
SORRY, AUNT VANN. UNCLE ABE GAVE ME A BOOK BEFORE HE DIED, AND I'M STILL NOT SURE IF IT'S REAL OR A WORK OF FICTION.
ABE NEVER CARED MUCH FOR FICTION. WHEN HE WAS LITTLE, HE DIDN'T NEED A FANTASY WORLD FOR FUN.
FOR HIM IT WAS HISTORY. REAL HISTORY, NOT THE B.S. THEY BARELY TEACH IN SCHOOL.
HE USED TO GET IN SO MUCH TROUBLE DIGGING AROUND OLD, ABANDONED LIBRARIES AND BOOKSTORES.
YOU'RE RIGHT. UNCLE ABE ONLY DEALT WITH FACTS.

WHICH MAKES THIS ALL THE MORE TERRIFYING.
I HATE TO ASK, BUT DO YOU THINK YOU CAN HELP PAY FOR THE FUNERAL EXPENSES? MONEY IS KIND OF TIGHT.
OF COURSE I'LL HELP, BUT WHAT ABOUT ABE'S ESTATE?
IT'S ALL GONE. HE LIQUIDATED HIS ASSETS BEFORE HE DIED.
SO WHERE DID ALL THE MONEY GO?
HE SPENT IT ON US!

TA-DA!
MR. NICHOLAS KNOX, YOUR UNCLE HIRED US TO PROTECT YOU.

NIXX INDUSTRIES, ROOF.
IT WILL BE AN HONOR KILLING YOU IN THE RING.
FUCK YOU. LET'S FIGHT.
LOOK AT THEM. THEY SCREAM FOR BLOOD. OUR BLOOD. THERE IS NOTHING PURER THAN RAW COMBAT. ONE OF US MUST DIE SO THAT THE WORLD CAN BE REBORN, JACK.
FUCK YOU. LET'S FIGHT.
GOD SPOKE TO ME AND SAID THAT TODAY ONE OF HIS MANY PROPHECIES SHALL BE FULFILLED.
FUCK YOU! LET'S FIGHT!!!
FINE! PUT 'EM UP, MOTHERFUCKER!!!

UGHH!
AHHHHH!
JUST LET GO AND CLOSE YOUR EYES, JACK!
YOU CAN'T FIGHT THE FUTURE!
ACKKK!
AHHHH! SON OF A BITCH!!!
BAM!

CONNECTICUT AVE NW, WASHINGTON, D.C.
WELCOME HOME, NICK!
HOME? I CAN'T STAY HERE. I JUST CAME TO FIND OUT WHY MY UNCLE HIRED YOU. WHO ARE YOU SUPPOSED TO BE PROTECTING ME FROM?
THEY'RE CALLED THE FINITES. THEY'RE AN ANCIENT CULT THAT'S INFILTRATED BUSINESSES, GOVERNMENTS, AND ORGANIZED RELIGIONS THE WORLD OVER.
AND YOU AND YOUR UNCLE HAVE A COPY OF THEIR BIBLE--A BLUEPRINT FOR THE END OF THE WORLD AND HOW TO REMAKE IT IN THEIR IMAGE.
I'M SORRY, THIS IS A LOT TO PROCESS. DO YOU HAVE ANY PROOF?

LOOK, WE ARE THE PROOF.
WE'VE DONE A FEW JOBS FOR THEM HERE AND THERE.
NOW CUT THE SHIT.
LOOK, YOUR UNCLE PAID US A SMALL FORTUNE TO HELP YOU SAVE THE WORLD.
PERSONALLY, I DON'T GIVE A DAMN. WE GETS PAID EITHER WAY.
SO ARE YOU IN?
OR ARE YOU OUT?
I'M IN. TELL ME EVERYTHING.

UGH. YOU SHOULD BE THANKING ME.
UHH
UGHH
KRRAK
ACK!
ADMIT IT!
YOU HAVEN'T FELT THIS ALIVE IN 20 YEARS!

IT'S BECAUSE YOU'RE FIGHTING FOR SOMETHING! IT MAKES YOU STRONG!
BUT I'M STILL GONNA GUT YOUR WIFE AND KID!
KRAAK!
WE'RE GOING TO CHANGE EVERYTHING, JACK.
SHUT UP!
SHUT UP!
SHUT UP!
SHUT UP!
SHUT UP!

WOOOO!

SHUT THE FUCK UP!!!

JUST SHUT--THE--FUCK--UP!
A MAN JUST DIED, AND YOU SICK MOTHERFUCKERS SIT IN THE STANDS AND CHEER?
YEAH, I KILLED 'IM, BUT AT LEAST I FEEL SOMETHING.
YOU PEOPLE LET US RULE YOU FROM THESE STUMPS! WE LIE TO YOU, GIVE YOU SHITTY HEALTH CARE, DEPRIVE YOU OF LITERACY, AND FORCE YOU TO PAY US ON APRIL 15TH TO DO IT.
WHAT THE FUCK IS WRONG WITH YOU?! WHAT THE FUCK IS WRONG WITH US?!
I DIDN'T WIN SHIT, FOLKS. I THINK I JUST BECAME A PART OF SOMETHING SO MUCH WORSE.
SO IF YOU WANT TO CHEER, WAVE FLAGS AND STAY UNINFORMED, BE MY FUCKING GUEST. I MAY HAVE DONE THE WRONG THING TODAY BUT AT LEAST I DID SOMETHING.
OPEN YOUR EYES AND DO SOMETHING!
BUT PLEASE DON'T CHEER FOR THIS.
WE ALL LOST TODAY.

HE LOOKS SO PEACEFUL.
DO YOU HAVE ANY IDEA HOW WEIRD THIS IS, MIMMS?
HE'S AN ABOMINATION. YET I CAN'T LOOK AWAY.
A LOT OF FIGHTERS WILL BE STUMPING FOR A SHOT AT THE WHITE HOUSE. WILL *HE* BE READY TO DEFEND HIS TITLE?
MAYBE. THE DRUGS MAKE HIM STRONGER, BUT THEY WEAKEN HIS HEART AND COGNITIVE ABILITIES.
I SAW MY FORMER STATE SENATOR JACK HAMMER WIN ON THE STUMP TODAY.
I MUST ADMIT I'M A BIT SURPRISED, YOLANDA. I WAS SURE THUNDER WOULD KILL HIM.
SO WAS I. BUT IT DOESN'T MATTER. SOMEONE DIED IN THE RING, AND THE VIEWS WERE IN THE BILLIONS. THE SLAY ACT WILL PASS.
THUNDER BEARER WON'T SEE PARADISE WITH US, BUT HE'LL BE REMEMBERED AS THE BELIEVER THAT HELPED TAKE US THERE.
YES, WE'VE WAITED FOR THIS DAY FOR A LONG TIME. LET US PRAY.
MAY WAR, FIRE, DEATH, AND THE BEASTS OF BABEL RETURN TO THIS LOST WORLD AND USHER IN THE REBIRTH OF ORDER, PEACE, AND PARADISE.

AMEN.

★ THE END ★

IN THE ARENA

IN RETROSPECT: THE ARENA IS BLOODY

JULIAN CHAMBLISS

When I wrote the first introduction to *In the Arena* back in 2019, I said I thought this project was about the difference between knowledge and information. We have information about our world, but can we craft it into knowledge we can act upon? I hoped that the backmatter essays in ON THE STUMP would allow people to see connections and imagine possibilities. In the months that followed, a global pandemic and grassroots protests for black lives have transformed our social landscape. At this writing, we cannot say the politics that guide our nation have risen to these challenges. The United States leads the world in COVID-19 deaths. Our elected officials seem unable or unwilling to address an epidemic of violence that claims black lives. What will be the outcome? It would be foolish to predict, but of course, I believe ON THE STUMP offers some framework to understand.

At its heart, ON THE STUMP is an Afrofuturist story. Kodwo Eshun, author of *More Brilliant Than The Sun: Adventures In Sonic Fiction* (1998), one of the earliest explorations of Afrofuturism, writes that Afrofuturism is, "... a program for recovering the histories of counter-futures created in a century hostile to Afrodiasporic projection and as space within which the critical work of manufacturing tools capable of intervention within the current political dispensation may be undertaken."[1] The interventions in the pages of ON THE STUMP are many. We should probably consider it as an example of black speculative practice. As such, this is a creative work that highlights the value of telling future stories from a black perspective. In 1994 Mark Dery, the scholar who coined the term Afrofuturism in his essay "Black to the Future," called our attention to the fact that, "African-American voices have other stories to tell about culture, technology, and things to come." He stressed we must seek Afrofuturism in "unlikely places" and "far-flung points." He placed the greatest emphasis on "black-written and black-drawn comics."[2]

Dery's call remains essential for us to consider. The scholars who contributed to the backmatter essays for ON THE STUMP were able to use the comic to say things about our world. A black ideology of freedom inspires Afrofuturist stories, but the tools for seeing what they offer matters to us all. This story, like so many Afrofuturist tales, highlights how oppressed people must imagine a better tomorrow. The stakes have risen in the short time we have been involved in this project, but the value for you as readers is to use the counter-future practice in the pages of ON THE STUMP to see the world anew.

Can you?

FIGHTING OVER AMERICA

MICHAEL D. KENNEDY

Political parties in the USA offer radically different visions of America, especially following the 2016 election. But what exactly they stand for depends on where you stand.

As I write, at least 20 contenders seek the Democratic Party's nomination to run for president. Pundits struggle to identify the contest's axes of difference. Is it a debate over how far left the party's policies will be? How do race, region, gender and generation figure in identifying the best candidate? Or should this decision be only pragmatic? Should Democrats base their decision on who is best equipped to beat Donald Trump and to flip the Senate to the Democrats? Many if not all Democrats believe that the Party must save the nation from an authoritarian who has violated its norms, if not also its laws. Has he burned its soul?

For those who saw a Black president as the source of their woe, however, Trump offered a salve for their resentment. Much like fans of professional wrestling who know it's not all real, but still love it, Trump's supporters look past his lies, crimes, and misdemeanors. He may be crude and erratic, but he stands opposed to a demon they call "political correctness." His Supreme Court appointments promise to undo laws assuring women's right to choose and other politics of equality and liberation. He doesn't brandish guns like he does golf clubs, but he stands with

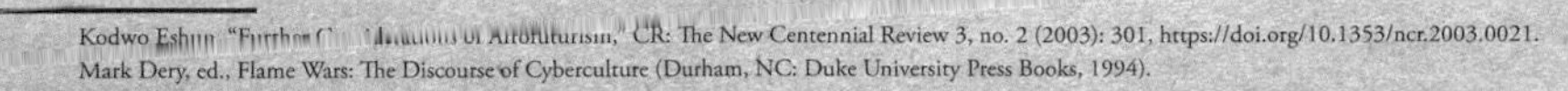

1 Kodwo Eshun, "Furthe[illegible] of Afrofuturism," CR: The New Centennial Review 3, no. 2 (2003): 301, https://doi.org/10.1353/ncr.2003.0021.
2 Mark Dery, ed., Flame Wars: The Discourse of Cyberculture (Durham, NC: Duke University Press Books, 1994).

the National Rifle Association, and they with him. He wants to "Make America Great Again" by building a wall to keep out Brown people and by forcing American manufacturers to build their goods at home, even if Trump-branded products are made in China.

Contradictions abound in Trumplandia, but that doesn't matter, even for his purported Party. Once self-understood as the party advocating free trade and national security, Trump has redefined the GOP to be his party, not a party of principle. He decries his predecessors' bad trade deals and the costs of being the world's policeman. He loves authoritarians in Russia, North Korea, Saudi Arabia and elsewhere more than traditional democratic allies, especially if they are women.

Women are fighting back, but the #MeToo movement does not seem to dent Trump's authority or affect his Supreme Court nominations. It has led to women's extraordinary political mobilization, however. Already in 2018, Democrats took back the House of Representatives with an unprecedented number of women and people of color in their ranks. While the measure of fury members of this new majority offer depends on their district's politics, cries of impeachment cascade and drown the cautions old guards offer.

Trump welcomes the attack. He ignores subpoenas and political norms, turning political pluralism away from a fight with rules to one with no holds barred. Racist dog whistles shift a struggle for political authority into a contest over defining the color of America. It's ugly, and has been bloody, and it could get worse, especially if 2020's election results are not overwhelming. America approaches a new kind of civil war if it does not invent a new America.

It is difficult to anticipate a United States of America. It feels like it is already lost. Belligerence replaces engagement, posturing supplants policies, and tweets trump insight. But the history of the USA is nothing if not unprecedented. Imagining new cultural politics for the times in which we live is not only possible, but necessary if we are to survive our planet's degradation and our world's brutalization. What vision and practice will tie us together in love for common future? Steel chairs may be more evident, but care, truth and beauty might still inspire us to fight for America, and not just over it.

THE FORGING OF A NATION

MATTHEW TEUTSCH

Francesco Chiappara's opening panel of ON THE STUMP [#1] shows an aerial view of the National Mall, looking towards the Washington Monument. Senators Jack Hammer and Sweet Smell Shaw prepare for their fight and stand on a large wooden stump in the foreground, the space where the Lincoln Memorial should be. This opening, with the visual focus of the stump-ring residing in the shadow of the Washington Monument, speaks to broader questions about national memory. While the comic's world seems fantastic, the opening image of ON THE STUMP joins a legacy of Black literature that confronts the exploitation that warped the shape of U.S. society and resonates with debates about race and justice.

In issue #2, Anna and Jack enter the Blacksmiths' Forge underneath the United States Capitol. As Jack opens the door, Anna asks him why they're at the Capitol, and he responds, "The building was built by slaves who would become the first Blacksmiths in 1863." The Forge serves as a space where the invisible becomes visible. It is a space that directly counters Senate Majority Leader Mitch McConnell's comments about reparations when he said, "I don't think reparations for something that happened 150 years ago for whom none of us currently living are responsible is a good idea." The Forge, with its placement below the Capitol, its classrooms, its training facilities, and its appearance as a Black history museum, shows that the legacy of slavery continues in the systems that undergird our nation.

In his 1829 Appeal to the Coloured Citizens of the World, David Walker points out the hypocrisy inherent in claiming that America rose up through hard work, an up-by-your-bootstraps mentality, and individuality. He highlights that these myths included immigrants from Greece, Ireland, and elsewhere who would assimilate into Whiteness, and he asks, "Have they not made provisions for the Greeks, and Irish? Nations who have never done the least thing for them, while we, who have enriched this country with our blood and tears—have

dug up gold and silver for them and their children, from generation to generation, and are in more miseries than any other people under heaven, are not seen, but by comparatively, a handful of the American people?" The Blacksmiths exist in the same way. While the FBI has a file on them, it is very small, and Anna even states that "[m]ost people don't even think they're real." They exist, as the enslaved men and women who Walker references, in almost complete obscurity because people do not choose to recognize them.

Ta-Nehisi Coates made this tension clear in his rebuttal to McConnell's comments during Congressional testimony when he stated, "... if Thomas Jefferson matters, so does Sally Hemmings. That if D-Day matters, so does Black Wall Street..." We cannot pick and choose the historical events we want to remember; we must remember all of them. We must rectify America's sin, and that is what the Blacksmiths work to do. ON THE STUMP makes a similar commentary through Anna when she tells Jack what she knows about the Blacksmiths, specifically that they "break the law and teach unlicensed minorities to read." While Anna is Black as well, she feels the need to uphold the laws that continue to keep "minorities" in submission. To this statement, Jack references slave laws forbidding enslavers to teach enslaved individuals to read, and he points out the current "literacy laws are actually based on income level. So, the Blacksmiths will teach anyone, not just minorities." The law denies these individuals access to literacy, and the Blacksmiths, like activists during the Antebellum period, Reconstruction, Jim Crow, and beyond, challenge the biased law by teaching them how to read.

We do not know the entire story of the Blacksmiths yet, but we do know that they built this nation, built the Capitol, and they continue to educate future generations in that knowledge, training them to combat a system that deems them invisible. ON THE STUMP enters into a long legacy of literature that deconstructs our national myths and reveals the truth about the ghosts of Black bodies that form the foundations of America, allowing them a voice and presence in our national memory.

RELIGION & POLITICS IN *ON THE STUMP*

MARTIN LUND

"Religion and politics."

Between you and me, I hate that phrase. It implies that what some of us call "religion" and politics are somehow separate entities and that "religion" is somehow above the fray of the muddled everyday. Hell, I don't think such a thing as "religion" exists, independent of human cultural activity and politics.

That might sound strange, coming from a religion scholar. It's not. I'm not alone. The underlying (relevant) point is that "religion" is a constructed category, made up in a colonial setting where Christians (mostly Protestants) wanted to name and classify things they encountered. But why this theory in a comic book? Because, whether or not you agree with the basic premise above, you should at least be able to agree with the consequence: they who have the power to define have the power to control. And that becomes relevant here because, well, you've read the latest ON THE STUMP; Thunder Bearer brought "religion" to the table in what you can probably agree is an inescapably political comic.

We've seen this power to define and control intertwined with questions of "religion" again and again in U.S. history. Slaves were denied access to parts of the bible that speak of freedom, hearing instead about servitude. Catholics and Jews (along with African-Americans) were socially and politically marginalized at the hands of the KKK and its largely WASP membership. George W. Bush backpedaled on his initial framing of the still-ongoing "War on Terror" as a "crusade," but he never dropped the coded evangelical language that kept white Christian America in his corner. Arguably, those ideas helped set the stage for Donald Trump's racist language to rally evangelicals to his side.

This is not to say that the things we call "religion" are by necessity something bad. There were many devoted abolitionists who found the strength to speak up and keep going based on "faith." Many opponents of Jim Crow segregation used "faith" as a motivator for their work, with the Reverend Dr. Martin Luther King, Jr. as perhaps the most famous example, but far from the last. So it goes, to this very day. As I write this, Jewish

Americans are protesting the violence of ICE, Muslim Americans are taking a principled stand against a racist president, and the Christian Left is issuing a clarion call for mercy, to name a few examples.

Point is, "religion" isn't bad or good on its own; "religion" is what people make it into. It exists only in choices made, actions taken, words spoken. That's why, although dressed in the trappings of more "exotic" forms of what is commonly recognized as "religion," Thunder's beliefs aren't all that strange, what with their focus on beginnings, ends, and rebirth.

Since the 1970s, the so-called "Christian Right" has been a constant and vocal presence in the U.S. political landscape. It's not a unified movement, and it doesn't have a singular agenda. There's plenty of conflict between and within forms of conservative (mostly but not exclusively Evangelical Protestant) Christianity. But the drive is in the same direction: to make America Christian "again." Never mind the separation of church and state. Never mind the diversity of the nation. Never mind freedom of religion. The idea is that the U.S. is losing its supposed historical "Christian (Protestant) identity" and there's been a growing push against this that impinges on reproductive rights, civil liberties, and the public sphere, from the White House to public school boards. It's meant to maintain an old patriarchal and white supremacist status quo that is increasingly being challenged.

This push leads to violence—emotional, psychological, and physical, especially now with an increasingly emboldened and growing white supremacist phalanx. It leads to a shrinking social world and to a more oppressive culture. And, although it can be easy to forget that Christianity historically rests on an apocalyptic longing, the desire for many in power (or who are clamoring for it) is for a fiery, bloody end to the world. So, while Thunder might not exist, his "religion" represents something that is all too real, and more people need to push against it, ON THE STUMP and off.

AFTERWORD

KARLOS K. HILL

In Chuck Brown and Francesco Chiappara's ON THE STUMP, fighting is the ultimate arbiter in politics. In this world, individuals/groups who can violently impose their will over others are deemed by society as the best fit to lead. In ON THE STUMP, not only is politics as violence enthusiastically embraced by the masses, it is understood as just and rational. While The Stump's story world seems fantastical and even antithetical to the American political tradition in relation to people of color, ON THE STUMP's story world is eerily representative of the Black experience.

For much of American history, anti-Black political violence has been the norm especially during the Reconstruction (1865–1877), the Lynching Era (1880–1930), and the American Civil Rights Movement (1945–1968). Anti-Black political violence (in its many manifestations) has been and continues to be the chief means through which white supremacy is actualized and perpetuated. While particular examples of anti-Black political violence are numerous perhaps some of the most emblematic are the Colafax (LA) Massacre (1873), the Barnswell (SC) Massacre (1876), the murder of civil rights activist Medgar Evers (1963), the 16th Street Baptist Church bombing (1963), Bloody Sunday (1965), and the assassination of Dr. Martin Luther King (1968). Whereas ON THE STUMP's story world revolves around violent combat as the mechanism for resolving political disputes, the reality of anti-Black political violence is that it excluded Black people from politics and the political process.

While Black people organized grassroots and national campaigns to win public support for their rights to be in the public square, the response from white Americans, particularly white secret societies such as the Ku Klux Klan, was violence. Groups like the KKK used lynchings, targeted killings, beatings, and house/church bombings to silence Black people and white allies. The Stump's story harkens back to a political legacy where violence was glorified and embraced as legitimate.

White-on-Black mobs lynched approximately five thousand Black Americans and in many instances hundreds of white spectators gathered to witness these deaths. Whites who organized, participated, or attended lynchings

as spectators were rarely, if ever, held accountable. The common belief among whites that lynching Black people was a just and sensible way to respond to alleged Black criminality, or more generally Black political dissent, made a mockery of the law.

Yet, this practice let white Americans impose their political vision of American society upon Black Americans. The mobs of the past and the angry politics of today share deep affinities with the dystopian political culture represented in ON THE STUMP. Rather than a far-fetched sci-fi story, ON THE STUMP reminds us of a political legacy that claimed lives and stifled liberty. As we read this story, we should see in the characters the twisted practice we, as a nation, struggled to overcome. Lastly, we should ask ourselves who benefits when politics and violence mix.

GOING TO THE MAT OVER AMBROSIA SALAD: FOOD (IN)JUSTICE IN *ON THE STUMP*

EMILY J.H. CONTOIS

Noticeably saccharine and nutritionally wanting, the barren foodscape of ON THE STUMP (OTS) sprouts mostly sweet treats: bags of Skittles, half-eaten candy bars, and blue-diarrhea-inducing frosty cakes. Characters consume such items quickly and in public, without much ceremony or a whiff of commensality. Senator Jack Hammer's stark food life is also marked by a somewhat surprising treat: ambrosia salad.

In Greek mythology, ambrosia is the sweet and fragrant food of the gods. Served and consumed at banquets, it sustained immortality alongside sacrifices made by human worshippers, usually meat. The OTS political system similarly requires bloody sacrifice through the face-crunching, gut-busting measures of the legislative process. Rather than eternal life, however, OTS's ambrosia offers a quick and fleeting sugar high.

The Greek God Grub food truck serves ambrosia salad, but it is reduced from heavenly fare to earthly fuel and sustenance rather than godly feasting and gastronomic pleasure. Ambrosia in OTS doesn't offer immortality, but the food truck's signage promises "all ambrosia" well into the night, much like "open till late" fast food restaurants. Such food is typically quick, convenient, affordable, and available. It can taste pretty good in the moment, but it still introduces a complicated bargain into our food lives when it comes to issues of longer-term health and sustainability.

Ambrosia salad is a somewhat odd choice for a dystopian food truck menu item. The fruity dessert began appearing in cookbooks in the nineteenth century, typically calling for oranges, sugar, and coconut. At the time, ambrosia salad represented an exotic luxury, as the expanding national food and transportation systems ensured steadier supplies of rare, harder to find ingredients like citrus. While some chefs today devise ambrosia salad with simple, fresh preparations, many recipes call for a host of highly processed ingredients: bagged mini marshmallows or marshmallow fluff or Jell-O mixed with canned orange slices, pineapple chunks, grated coconut, and maraschino cherries laced with Red 40 dye.

No matter how it's prepared, ambrosia salad remains for some eaters a traditional and meaningful holiday dish, particularly for Christmas in the Southern U.S. Conversely, Hammer eats ambrosia salad alone, quickly, and messily, as he slurps and squishes the syrupy concoction directly from a large bowl. Mirroring the spike and fall of insulin levels, the rushed and sometimes desperate consumption of sugary foods in OTS maps the action of the narrative, as it vacillates between moments of intense violence.

Sugary, processed foods pose no problem on their own. Writing this essay has motivated me to make and try my first ambrosia salad. But food systems primarily composed of limited, processed, high-sugar options pose a threat to community food justice, sovereignty, health, and longevity. For many, securing access to nutritious, affordable and culturally appropriate food is a daily struggle, one that disproportionately affects low income communities of color. While ON THE STUMP's violent political process may seem like an exaggeration of our own world, the inequities of our current food system are not far removed from these bombastically sugary tales. That's something worth going to the mat over.

JULIAN C. CHAMBLISS is Professor of English and the Val Berryman Curator of History at the MSU Museum at Michigan State University. He is a core participant in the MSU College of Arts & Letters' Consortium for Critical Diversity in a Digital Age Research (CEDAR). His research interests focus on race, identity, and power in real and imagined spaces. Chambliss is co-producer and host of *Every Tongue Got to Confess*, a podcast examining communities of color. Also, he is a producer and host of *Reframing History*, a podcast exploring history theory and practice in the United States. Follow him on Twitter: @JulianChambliss

MICHAEL D. KENNEDY is professor of sociology and international and public affairs at Brown University. His research interests include the sociology of knowledge and universities, global transformations, social movements, and solidarity within and across nations. His most recent book, *Globalizing Knowledge: Intellectuals, Universities and Publics in Transformation* (Stanford University Press, 2015) addresses those themes. Follow him on Twitter @Prof_Kennedy.

MATTHEW TEUTSCH is the Director of the Lillian E. Smith Center at Piedmont College. He is the editor of Rediscovering *Frank Yerby: Critical Essays* (University Press of Mississippi, 2020). His publications have appeared in *CLA Journal*, *MELUS*, *Mississippi Quarterly*, and *Studies in the Literary Imagination*. He is a regular contributor to *Black Perspectives* and *Teaching United States History*. His research focuses on African American, Southern, and Nineteenth-Century American literature. He maintains *Interminable Rambling*, a blog about literature, composition, culture, and pedagogy. His current project is a monograph examining Christopher Priest's run on Black Panther (1998-2003).

MARTIN LUND is senior lecturer in religious studies at Malmö University in Sweden. Among his main research interests are the intersections of religions and comics. He has written about Jack Chick's propaganda comics, among other things, so Thunder Bearer's message is familiar to him.

KARLOS K. HILL is Chair of and Associate Professor in the Clara Luper Department of African and African-American Studies at the University of Oklahoma. He is author of *Beyond the Rope: The Impact of Lynching on Black Culture and Memory* (Cambridge University Press, 2016) as well as author of the forthcoming book *The Murder of Emmett Till: A Graphic History* (Oxford University Press, Summer 2020).

EMILY J.H. CONTOIS is an Assistant Professor of Media Studies at The University of Tulsa. She is the author of *Diners, Dudes & Diets: Gender & Power in U.S. Food Culture & Media*, out fall 2020 from UNC Press, and co-editor of the forthcoming volume *Food & Instagram: Identity, Influence & Resistance*. She teaches courses on food media, advertising, and popular culture, writes for *Nursing Clio*, and blogs at emilycontois.com. She holds a PhD in American Studies from Brown University, an MLA in Gastronomy from Boston University, and an MPH focused in Public Health Nutrition from University of California, Berkeley. Twitter: @emilycontois

★ CHARACTER DESIGNS ★

ANNA

When designing Annabelle Lister, we wanted her to have a toned, muscular physique. She's a well trained FBI agent with a strong personality and a sharp sense of justice. Anna never holds back when it's time to land a solid punch! She is slender and agile, a look Prenzy achieved by keeping her clothing simple; a tank top, ripped jeans and long boots—classic badass attire! The denim jacket was also a deliberate choice. It adds a sense of movement to Anna's form during her many action scenes.

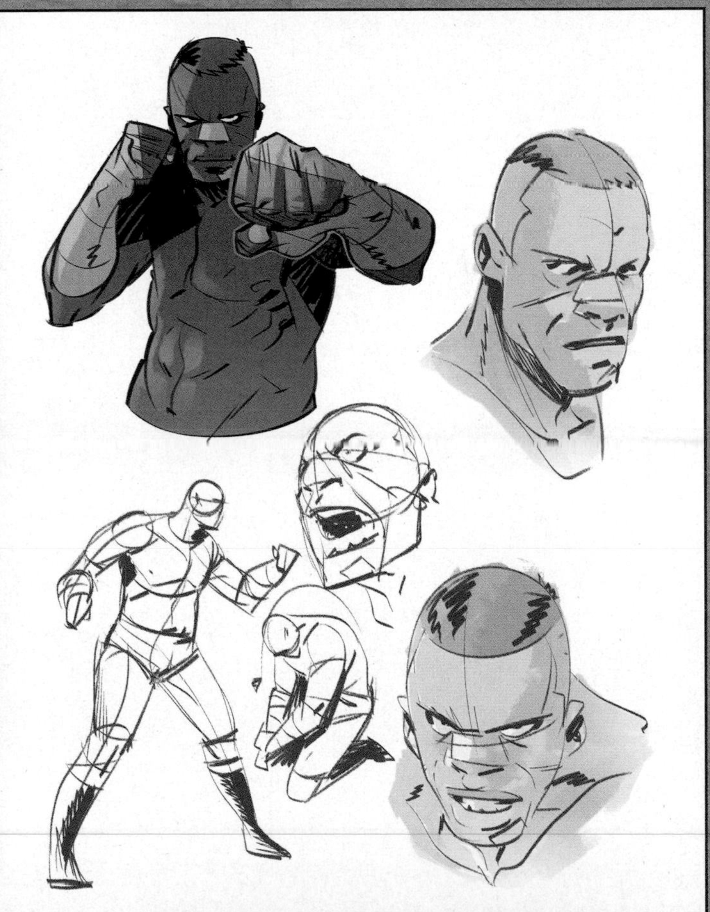

JACK

While most senators stop fighting when they hit forty, Jack Hammer is still plugging along well into his fifties! His physique is robust and fairly muscular—but he still has a bit of a belly. In this way, Jack is shaped more like an old, tired wrestler than an active fighter. Even in Prenzy's preliminary character sketches, the decades of struggle and pain were clearly visible on his face. One of Jack's main character traits is using his sharp wit and sarcasm to mask his inner turmoil.

GABRIEL

Superior Court Judge Gabriel Horn leads the DC Blacksmiths with his daughter Nat as second in command. The pair are both nimble expertly trained fighters with lean builds. Gabe's long beard hangs over the hollow wrinkles in his face, making him look wise and experienced.

NAT

Nat Horn is youthful and agile, which easily enables her to sneak up on unsuspecting targets. Though she lacks her father's experience, Nat is determined and eager for systemic change. She never misses an opportunity to let Gabriel know how they could be doing more to teach the marginalized to read, write, and fight!

THUNDER BEARER

Thunder Bearer is a powerful senator with an inflated sense of self and a low threshold for defiance. He believes that his destiny is to foster a new era made in the image of a nefarious cult. Thunder's main ambition is passing the Slay Act, a brutal piece of legislation that would legalize death matches on the stump and effectively throw society further into chaos. His design integrates the threatening presence of a Norse viking with the overwhelming brawniness of a robust woodsman. Thunder's belt transforms into a flying guillotine which he uses to decapitate his foes before collecting their heads as trophies.

MADAME MAYHEM

An expert in hand-to-hand combat and several weapons, Madame Mayhem is one of few assailants capable of holding their own against Anna and Nat. On top of her excellence as a seasoned fighter, Mayhem is also a shrewd businesswoman and a trusted member of Thunder's inner circle. She is the owner of a seedy nightclub that serves as a protective veneer for corrupt government secrets, in addition to catering Washington's elite. Mayhem was designed to have a strong, lithe build which enables her to move with speed and accuracy. Her personal uniform consists of leather bodysuits, stockings, and chunky combat boots.

JOE

Joe Doakes is a deranged, clown-faced bruiser with a twisted smile and a sadistic disposition. He has a thick, sturdy physique, which enables him to take a great deal of punishment without sustaining too much damage. He's basically a tank! Joe has long since left the gay conversion camp where he was trained as a mercenary, but he still chooses to wear the program's signature "clown soldier" make-up. He does this as a silent protest against the program's overt cruelty and to honor the lives lost under its authority.

CAM

Working for both government entities and private sector interests, Cam is a foul-mouthed, hot-blooded hired gun without any regard for authority. In fact, she would turn on her employer in a second if the opposing side seemed more fun. Cam is loud and impulsive, often looking to her more demure professional partner Kay Cee for balance and stability. Her interest in illegal genetic enhancement is only made evident by the scales on her arms and her viciously sharp canines. These recreational mutations also affect her physical abilities, making her more robust and faster than most other human beings.

KAY CEE

Level headed and professional, Kay Cee operates as a calm, calculated mercenary, executing plans with surgical precision. In contrast to Cam's often manic behavior, she is exceptionally low-key, never uses profanity, and often shows no emotion at all. Though her personality is much more reserved than her partner's, Kay Cee is just as deadly. Her composure is simply a method of controlling her lethality. She is a skilled assassin with extensive military training, after all. Her friendship with Cam is one of the few things keeping her tethered to sanity. Without her, Kay Cee would likely snap.